This Ladybird book

belongs to

_____

A catalogue record for this book is available from the British Library

Published by Ladybird Books Ltd
27 Wrights Lane London W8 5TZ
A Penguin Company
2 4 6 8 10 9 7 5 3 1
© LADYBIRD BOOKS LTD MM

Printed in Italy

Snuggle down
ducklings

by Mandy Ross
illustrated by Jo Brown

Ladybird

"Bedtime, my little ducklings," quacked Mother Duck.

So after one last dibble-dabble, the little ducklings dibble-dabbled home to their nest in the reeds.

"Will she be coming soon?" they quacked.

"As soon as the moon," nodded Mother Duck.

Then with a quack and a kiss
and their feathers tucked tight,
the ducklings snuggled down in
their nest for the night.

And they waited...

"Bedtime, my little fishes,"
glubbed Father Fish.

So after one last swishy-swim,
the little fishes swishy-swam
home to their reedbed
under the banks.

"Will she be coming soon?"
they glubbed.

"As soon as the moon,"
nodded Father Fish.

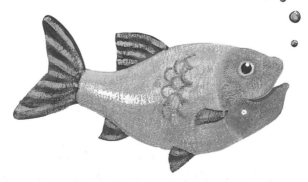

Then with a swish and a kiss
and their fins tucked tight,
the fish snuggled down in the
reedbed for the night.

And they waited…

"Bedtime, my little froggies,"
croaked Grandmother Frog.

So after one last leggy-leapfrog,
the little frogs leapfrogged
home to their waterlily leaf.

"Will she be coming soon?"
they croaked.

"As soon as the moon,"
nodded Grandmother Frog.

*Then with a croak and a kiss
and their webbed feet tucked tight,
the frogs snuggled down on a
lily for the night.*

And they waited…

…until the moon rose over the willow trees.

"Listen," quacked the ducklings. "Listen," glubbed the fish. "Listen," croaked the frogs.

And then they heard the moonbird swooping by, singing softly,

"Hush-a-bye, ducklings, froggies and fish. Snuggle to sleep as the waters go swish…

The moon and the stars are silvery bright, and you will have silvery dreams tonight."

And all night long the ducklings, the frogs and the fish dreamed their swishy, silvery dreams under the moon and stars.

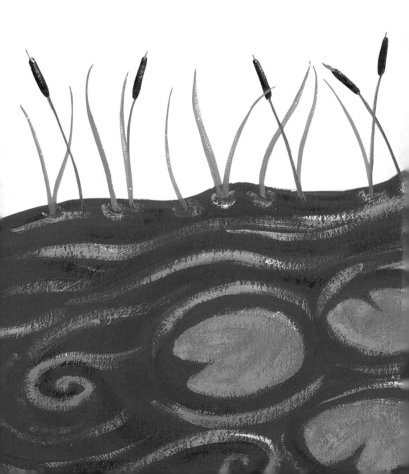